THE NEW BIZARRO AUTHOR SERIES

PRESENTS

MUSCLE MEMORY

STEVE LOWE

Thanks for the support, Steven!
[signature]

Eraserhead Press
Portland, OR

THE NEW BIZARRO AUTHOR SERIES
An Imprint of Eraserhead Press

ERASERHEAD PRESS
205 NE BRYANT
PORTLAND, OR 97211

WWW.ERASERHEADPRESS.COM

ISBN: 1-936383-01-2

Printed in the USA.

You hold in your hands now a book from the New Bizarro Author Series. Normally, Eraserhead Press publishes twelve books a year. Of those, only one or two are by new writers. The NBAS alters this dynamic, thus giving more authors of weird fiction a chance at publication.

For every book published in this series, the following will be true: This is the author's first published book. We're testing the waters to see if this author can find a readership, and whether or not you see more Eraserhead Press titles from this author is up to you.

The success of this author is in your hands. If enough copies of this book aren't sold within a year, there will be no future books from the author published by Eraserhead Press. So, if you enjoy this author's work and want to see more in print, we encourage you to help him out by writing reviews of his book, telling your friends, and giving feedback at www.bizarrocentral.com.

In any event, hope you enjoy…

—Kevin L. Donihe, Editor

This is for Michele. We still laugh together.

Also, big thanks go to the helpful ladies and gents at Zoetrope and Seven Deadly Pens, particularly one Kevin Wallis. You rock, dude.

PART ONE

The Ol' Switcheroo

I SHOULDA KNOWN something was up when the dog meowed at me.

He's standing next to the bed. Don't quite understand what he's trying to tell me, what with the skittish little mews slipping out of his drooling muzzle. It shoulda been downright disconcerting to hear that coming from an English Mastiff named Demolisher.

But I'm in that in between. Halfway into wakefulness, but still halfway down in the deepest sleep I can remember. I'm standing at the toilet, trying to fish my hog out before I piss all over the place. It takes me a minute to realize my nightgown ain't got a dickhole in it. So I do what any red-blooded man does when he's a little wobbly in the morning and is wearing a nightgown without a dickhole.

I drop my panties around my ankles and sit down to pee.

You do it, too, so don't even play that bullshit with me. You pop a squat when it's handy to do so. Only problem is, getting up outta the warm bed, everything's relaxed and hanging low, you usually have to hike up the travelers so they don't go for an early morning dip. Am I right?

So here I am, fishing between my legs for my balls and not having much success. Little Rico starts crying and my tits instantly start to ache and the front of my nightgown soaks through. Nipples hard as rocks and ringing with the vibrations from his hungry little cry.

Right there, I realize I'm reaching between my legs for nothing. Grabbing air where the boys should be swinging. My hog, he ain't down there either.

9

You know those What the Fuck moments you get from time to time, when shit is so backwards and out of whack, all you can do is step back and go, What the Fuck? Yeah, that's what this is.

Let's just kinda skip over this next part, 'cause really it's just me running around and shrieking and freaking out over the sound of my shrieking and then realizing that I'm still in bed, but not really 'cause here I am standing in front of a two hundred-pound meowing horse of a dog, and not really understanding any of it until I look in the mirror and see Tina in the reflection, only it's me, and I think I may have lost my dick in the toilet and my tits hurt and my nightgown is soaked around the nipples with cold milk 'cause Rico is raising a fuss, but all the while I see me, see myself just lying there in the bed not moving, which is usually the thing I do when Little Rico starts to cry, just pretend that I'm asleep so I don't have to go get him. I mean what's the point when Tina's got to feed him anyways? I mean it's not like I have tits of my own, except this morning, when all of a sudden I seem to have tits of my own.

Right.

So I'm sitting at the kitchen table. Or, Tina's sitting at the table, but I see what she sees. I am Tina. Sort of. And I got Little Rico and I'm trying to feed him and I have the hardest damn time figuring out how the hell to get a tit out of this nightgown without hiking it all the way up over my head. I have to pull my arm through the strap and damn near take the thing half off. And man, that little sucker clamps down on that nipple like nobody's business.

Tucker comes stumbling over from next door and he's standing in my kitchen. The screen door whips shut and whacks him in the ass, only it's not Tucker's ass, it's his wife Julia's ass. But I know it's Tucker in there 'cause he's got this look on her face just like what I got on mine. Or

I mean on Tina's.

I say, "Dude, you too?" and then I actually look over my shoulder for Tina. I'm not quite used to her voice coming out when I talk.

"What... The... Fuck... Is this?" Yep, that's Tucker.

So we're both sitting here at my kitchen table, and we're trying our damndest to figure this out. I mean, it's Julia sitting across from me, her voice and everything, but it's Tucker on the inside. He's (er, she's) drinking a beer while I try to nurse Rico. The little bastard is chewing the fuck outta my nipples, and the whole time Tucker/Julia is staring at my tits.

"Dude, do you mind? Not only are you eyeballing my tits...my *wife's* tits, but you're doing it while I'm trying to feed a goddamn baby."

"Sorry dude."

"So where is Julia? She *is* you now, right?"

"I don't rightly know. Last I seen her, she was screamin' my head off and runnin' around. Then she snatched up the car keys and went tear-assin' down the road."

Princess Diamond Roses snuggles up to Tucker's leg (which is really Julia's leg—you probably get the idea now, right?). He reaches down and strokes the cat behind its ears. Princess looks up at him and barks.

"Whoa."

"Yeah, no shit, whoa."

"So this is like one of them *Twilight Zone* things, right? Or maybe it's more like a Dark Matters or something."

"*Tales From the Dark Side.*"

"Yeah. That was the black and white one with the dude in the suit who kinda talked like Captain Kirk before Captain Kirk was on."

"No, that was *Twilight Zone.* That was Rod Serling. *Tales From the Dark Side* came after."

"Oh. Yeah."

He's staring at my tits again and guzzling his beer. It's starting to piss me off. That's when Julia, who's really Tucker now, comes in through the screen door. It bangs shut and whacks her (or him, I guess) in the ass.

"What the hell is this?" Julia's words coming out in Tucker's low, gravelly voice.

"Dude," says Tucker. "I know, right? What the hell, right?"

"Tucker, it's six in the morning and you're drinking a beer?"

"Fucks yeah I am."

"Do you not remember what beer does to me? It makes me bloated and gives me diarrhea. Hell-oooo?"

"Well, sucks to be you." He gives me one of them shit-eatin' grins, but then it hits him and he sits there looking at the bottle. "Oh. Yeah. Shit."

Julia takes a couple big, awkward, clomping steps over to the table and straddles a chair. "Jesus, Tuck, how the hell do you walk around with this thing between your legs?"

Tucker grins and nods his head. "That's what she said."

"Um, Tucker?" Julia's looking down at the crotch of her gym shorts. It's poking through the slats of the chair. "What the hell is this all about? You're getting a boner."

The other strap of my nightgown keeps slipping down and Tucker's looking at my tits again and his wife has a boner. And Little Rico bites my nipple so hard I shriek. "Fuck, Rico, take it easy on the software, dude!"

"You know, there's a flap on the front of your night-gown. For feeding the baby."

I guess I'm just staring at Julia kinda blank like, 'cause she rolls her eyes and walks around behind me. She helps me with my shoulder strap and reaches under my arm to undo the button. Her hands are big and rough and a little scratchy and she fumbles with it for a second. Then my tit flops out right there for Little Rico and he nuzzles up and keeps on eating. Julia's boner pokes me in the back of my neck.

"Oops. Shit. Sorry." She shoots a pissed look at Tucker, but he's rubbing his own nipples. Or rather, he's feeling up Julia's nipples. She says, "Stop that, dummy. You'll make 'em chafe."

"This is so trippy, dude." He takes another swig of beer and belches.

Julia shakes her head at him and says to me, "So how come Tina's not awake?"

That's a damn good question. I don't have an answer so I say, "That's a damn good question."

Rico's back to sleep now. The little parasite's done chewing me to shreds. I put him back in his crib and the three of us go into my bedroom and stand next to the bed and stare at my body. Nothing happening, at all. Mouth hanging half open, eyes still closed up tight. Tucker flicks my nose and says, "Yo! Billy! Wake up dude."

"Would you shut the fuck up? I just got Little Rico back to sleep. And besides, *I'm* fucking Billy. That's Tina now. Remember dumbass?"

"Oh. Yeah. Sorry."

I put a hand on my chest, er Tina's chest. Nothing. Julia puts two fingers alongside Tina's neck and looks at the ceiling for about a minute. Her eyes are all wide. "Oh my God. She's dead."

"She is?" I'm having a hard enough time getting this thing right in my brain, but now it's all a jumble again. "No, wait. She ain't dead. I'm dead. Right?"

The three of us just stand there catching flies for I don't know how long. Tucker's got this look on his face like he gets when somebody asks him for directions or if he has to do math. Then he's ticking things off on his fingers and mumbling.

13

"So, wait," he says. "You're dead, but you didn't die because now you're her. You're Tina. And Tina is you, so now Tina's dead. Because you died."

Julia turns without a word and heads out the room. Her boner brushes against my thigh. "Sorry," she says. "Goddammit Tucker, how do you turn this thing off?"

"Dude, go through last night for me. What happened before you went to bed? Do you remember feeling sick or anything?"

"Not really. I mean, I had a few beers and stuff, so you know how that goes. Me and Tina been fightin' a lot lately, but last night was OK. She was real nice and stuff."

"Billy, you should come out here." Julia's out in the kitchen. She's looking at the sink, at the empties littered in and around it. She's pointing at a yellow container on the counter.

Tucker grabs it up and reads the label. "Dude, how come you keep your antifreeze in the kitchen?"

You know that What the Fuck moment we talked about earlier? Well, this here is another one. Julia sniffs an empty beer bottle and dumps the little dribbles into the sink. Faint neon backwash drips out. She sets the bottle down and flips through the cabinets above the sink. "Where do you keep your medications?"

I guess I point to the cabinet at the end of the counter 'cause she goes down there and starts shuffling around the pill bottles. I can't stop looking at that glowing juice in the sink. Tucker's right there with me, both of us leaning over staring at it.

"Oh my God, dude. Did your wife try to kill you?"

"Uh. I guess so."

"But she didn't kill *you*. I mean, she did, but you weren't you when you died."

"Uh. Yeah, guess so."

"So, does that make it a murder *and* a suicide?"

"Billy… Billy!" Julia's got pill bottles sticking out of her Tucker man-hands and she shakes them at me. "Was Tina taking these?"

"Uh." I ain't the most reliable source for information right now.

"Haldol? Wellbutrin?"

"I don't know."

"Did she have post partum depression?"

Shit. I don't know. That should be something I would know, but I don't know. I just kinda look at Julia.

She tosses the pill bottles on the counter and hustles off to Little Rico's room. When I get in there, she's peeling back his eyelids and feeling his forehead. "Has he been acting normal?"

"Yeah, I guess. Geez, you don't think she poisoned the baby, too, do you?"

"No. She just killed you was all."

Well, that's a relief.

Tucker stands in the doorway holding his gut and says, "Oof. I think that beer just hit me." He runs off to the bathroom.

Julia leans out the door and shouts after him, "Make sure you wipe front to back! And don't go fiddling around down there! That don't belong to you, got it?"

* * *

Tucker's in the bathroom for a long time. Julia's pretty antsy, keeps looking down the hall at the door. Me, I'm just numb. My mind keeps swirling from one thing to the next, mixing it up, dumping it back out. In my head, I'm me. About six-feet-two and a couple hundred pounds worth of All American man. Ok, about two hundred and thirty pounds, I guess. But I look down at my thin fingers and my trembling hands and my quivering, engorged chest, and I just can't seem to make sense of it. The world before me starts to swim. Everything's shimmering and twinkly.

Julia snatches a tissue out of the box on the table and hands it to me. "I know, hon. It's gonna be alright."

"But it's not alright," I sob. And when I hear that sadness in my voice, it just makes me sadder. And then Little Rico starts to cry again and my tits immediately start to leak and that makes me cry even more.

"Welcome to the world of the woman."

Tucker finally stumbles out of the bathroom. He's a little wobbly in the knees. Julia shakes her head in disgust. "You asshole. I told you to leave me alone in there."

"Man." He's a little out of breath. "You ain't kidding that's hard to find. But, boy when you do…"

"Congratulations," Julia says. "Only took you seven years. Lot of good it does me now." She rubs at the front of her gym shorts, still poked straight out. She goes into Little Rico's room and brings him to me. She's got him cradled so gently in one of her big, hairy, tattooed arms. I cry some more at how cute they look.

"Here ya go little guy." She passes him over to me. I start to undo the button on my nightgown, but Julia says, "No, no, switch to the other one. You have to go back and forth." So I undo the other flap and Rico digs in. It still hurts, but this time is different. It feels better now. He's so warm and soft.

Julia hooks Tucker's arm and drags him over to the door. "We're gonna go, but if you need anything, anything at all, you call, OK? I'm just next door."

I snuffle up a gob of snot and shake my head yes and tears flip off of my eyelashes and splash on my arms. Julia pulls Tucker out the door. "Later, dude," he says.

I walk out to the front porch and stand there with Little Rico in my arms and watch the sun rise over the trees. I cry some more. Demolisher curls up at my feet and purrs in the warmth of the mounting sun.

A stray sheep from Edgar's house next door wanders into the yard. It stops and looks up at me and says, "Morning, ma'am."

"Edgar? Is that you?"

"Hey, hold on there. This ain't what you think it is."

* * *

"You alright little dude?"

Rico gurgles some baby talk and gags on a hiccup. Can't tell if he's looking up at me or at the canvass-wrapped dangly mirror thing waving across his face. Must be the mirror thing. I don't think his eyes focus out very far yet. Starts to get all cross-eyed when he tries to. Either way, he seems happy enough. Suppose I would be too if I could fill my pants like he just did and make somebody else wipe it up.

I can't just sit around. I'm done crying and now it feels like the walls are closing in on me. Too much weirdo shit happening to lie around and wait for answers. I flip on the baby monitor and grab the receiver out of the kitchen. Then I head over to Tucker's. The baby monitor crackles a little bit and, I swear to God, I think for a second that maybe it's aliens. Like from that movie by M. Night Shamalamadingdong, whatever the hell his name is. I actually lift the receiver up in the air and hold my breath for a second and listen.

"They're coming to get you Ba-a-a-a-rbara."

"Screw you, Edgar. I thought I told you before to keep your animals over on your own damn property. It's a good thing it's you in there, otherwise I'd be having mutton for dinner tonight."

"But you've got Kentucky bluegrass over here. And fescue. My yard's nothing but ragweed and dirt clods anymore." He leans over, tugs out a clump of ankle-high grass and chews.

"Why don't you just go get something normal to eat? Just 'cause you're a sheep, you gotta eat on grass?"

"I dunno. 'Cause grass is what sheep'r supposed to eat." He points a hoof at me and says, "And it's not like I'm gonna have an easy time taking lids off a cans and shit with these. Besides, it actually tastes OK. Kinda sweet. Funny thing is, I never was much for eatin' salads."

"Hey, if you're in there, where's, you know, *you*?"

I have to wait for him to chew up his grass to answer. "In the barn. She was going a little nuts at first and banging my body all around. Once I kinda figured out what was going on, I got the hell outta there and managed to push the barn door shut. Hopefully she's sleeping it off right now."

"Wait a sec," I say. "How exactly are you even talking to me?"

"Huh?" He cocks his sheep head at me like I'm speaking in French.

"Do sheep have voice boxes? Can they form actual human words?"

"Uh…"

You know what, not now. Too much else to deal with. "Never mind, Edgar. Feel free to dine on as much bluegrass as you want. Maybe then I won't have to mow the lawn anymore."

"That's mighty kind of you ma'am. Er, sir."

I keep on going to Tucker's. Just a short walk, still in the range of the baby monitor. Least I think Tina used to take it with her to see Julia sometimes. I yank open their screen door and get halfway into the kitchen and see 'em there. Tucker with his shirt off, tits and everything hangin' out in the breeze. Julia holding a bra up to him, showing him the clasp.

"Oh, damn. Sorry Julia. My bad."

"Nah, it's alright," Tucker says. "C'mon in. I don't mind. I was checking yours out before, only right that you get to sneak a peek at mine."

Julia raises a Tucker eyebrow at him and says, "What do you mean, 'mine'? Those aren't yours, dummy."

"Well, for the moment they seem to be in my possession, and if you plan to get 'em back in the same shape you left 'em in, I suggest you start being a little nicer. And stop callin' me dummy!"

"OK, sorry. I'll stop calling you dummy. You just don't understand it from a woman's point of view. Those are delicate, feminine things and they need to be handled with care. They're not your personal play toys, and you need to treat me with respect."

"Alright. I will. I might not completely understand yet, but I seem to be getting a crash course here. Gotta give me time to take it in is all. Now help me put this bra on. Your back is killing me."

"Maybe I'll just go since you guys—"

"No, it's OK," Julia says. "Come on in. We been doing some thinking and we might as well get your ideas."

I pull up a chair and watch the spectacle, despite myself. Tucker's tits are pretty big, bigger than I realized when they still officially belonged to Julia. Good thing she's here to show him how to work that bra, otherwise he'd probably hang himself trying to wrestle it on.

She gets it in place and tucks him in all nice and snug and tries to hook it in back but has a hell of a time.

"Jesus, Tuck, how do you do anything with these big, clumsy sausages?"

"I told you that shit ain't easy. They make them clasp things for ladies' fingers, not for Tucker's fingers."

"Yeah, I see what you mean."

I say, "So, you guys were thinking? About what the hell

mighta happened?"

Tucker cups his newly supported chest and tests the firmness. "Yeah," he says still looking down at himself. "They don't have much on the news yet. The TV station had a buncha folks call in sick on account of this shit and all they're saying right now is that the authorities advise everybody to stay home until something gets figured out. And then Edgar came over a while ago for some grass and he said... Wait, did you see Edgar?"

"Jesus, yeah, I saw him."

"Dude, I *told* you about that like six months ago. Didn't I? Didn't I tell you he was doing that with his livestock?"

"Yeah, so you were right. I owe you a case. But to get back to the important point here..."

"He said he saw a flash," Julia says. "Some time early in the morning. He was walking from his house out to his barn and saw a flash of blue light."

Tucker mumbles out the side of his mouth, "Shoulda asked him why he was heading to the barn at three in the morning."

"It doesn't matter, Tuck. He says he saw the flash, got to the barn, and that's it. He wakes up the next morning with lambs tugging at him for some breakfast."

Shit, maybe it *is* aliens. Tucker must be reading my mind.

"Dude, I'm thinking aliens," he says. "They fly down here, zap us with some goofy ray that somehow switches our minds into somebody else's body, maybe whoever we were closest to or in the same room with when it happened. You and Tina, me and Julia. Edgar and his wooly lover. Do your cat and dog sleep together? Never mind, doesn't matter." Tucker waves his hands around like he's directing landing aircraft. "And then, when we're all confused and running around and disoriented, that's when they hit us. When we're at our weakest. Like them stories Edgar's daddy used to go tellin' everybody 'round town."

Julia shakes her head and I can see the word dummy dancing on her tongue. "Tucker, if that was true, then wouldn't they be attacking us right now?"

Tucker glances around and peers out the windows. "Shit, yeah. You're right. Maybe we should get down to the basement."

I say, "Dude, calm down. It ain't aliens."

"How the hell do you know?"

"Because I do. It *ain't* aliens." I don't know who I'm trying to convince more here, him or me.

"Yeah? And aren't you the one who said Edgar wasn't doing you-know-what to his you-know-whats, too?"

"Hey! I wasn't doin' nothing to my sheep!" Edgar's got his nose pressed to the screen door, his two front hooves propped on the top porch step, patch of grass sticking out the side of his mouth.

Julia says, "Alright ladies, that's enough. Listen, why don't you go see if McGillicuddy's is open and do some investigating? See what other folks are saying." She points at Tucker and says, "And no more beer, got it?"

"Don't have to tell me twice. Let's go dude."

"But what about Little Rico? I can't just up and leave him."

"I got it, Billy, don't worry," she says. "Just leave me the baby monitor."

Don't have to tell me twice to go down to McSwillin-Buddies, either. We're gone.

"Billy!" Julia's standing in the door as we head toward Tucker's truck. "You guys still have all those old VHS tapes down in your basement?"

I flip down the tailgate and help Edgar climb up into the bed. "Yeah, sure. Help yourself. Couldn't sell a one of 'em last yard sale we had. Whatcha wanna watch them for?"

"Research."

* * *

We walk into McSwillinBuddies nice and slow, not quite sure what we're gonna find in there. The bright mid-morning light from the open door shines in on four vaguely familiar female faces. The bartender, an overweight woman with a jumbled mess of unnatural, jet-black hair points at us and says, "We don't serve their kind here."

She's pointing at Edgar. "Your sheep, he'll have to wait outside."

"Man, I ain't really a sheep. I'm Edgar."

She looks at him with wide eyes. "Edgar Winter? What the hell you doin' in there?"

Tucker says, "Danny Boy? Is that you?"

"Yeah. Who's askin'?"

"It's Tucker and Billy. And Edgar the sheep."

"Damn, boys, come on in and grab a stool. Didn't recognize you on account of the circumstances."

We slap the dull, worn bust of Terry Bradshaw mounted next to the door and say, "Go Steelers," like we always do when we come to McSwillinBuddies. Danny Boy sets two beers on the bar for us. Edgar snorts at the Bradshaw bust and says, "Yo, what about me?"

Tucker says, "Can I get a bowl for our woolen friend here?"

Danny Boy dumps pretzels out of a bar bowl and hands it to Tucker. Then he says in a lowered voice, "Goddamn Tucker, you was right about Edgar."

"Man, what the hell have you been telling everybody about me?"

Tucker pours his beer into the bowl and sets it on the floor for Edgar. "What? Nothing. Just drink your beer, dude."

"Keep talkin' shit about me and I'm gonna bite your ass." He mumbles something about giving all of us the sheep flu and shoves his snout in the bowl, slopping beer onto the floor.

I look down the bar at the three ladies watching us. As if on cue, they raise their hands one at a time and introduce themselves.

"Hey Billy, Joe Vickers here." Old looking blonde in bad need of a fresh dye job.

"'Sup Billy? It's Landis." Skinny chick with a light moustache and tattooed letters on the fingers of her right hand that spell out L A D Y. I got ten to one that the fingers on her other hand say F O X Y. And then I shudder at the thought.

"Floyd Roundtree." A pretty hot redhead holding up a glass of whiskey. Everybody shoots glances at Floyd. I don't think none of us can believe that a sloppy dude like him could be married to such a good lookin' woman.

Sitting at a table behind us is Karl. He's all alone, like usual, got his standard Cutty and water in hand. I say, "Karl? Is that really you?"

"Yeah," he says. Kinda spits it out. "I'm just fine. Alone, as always." He throws back the rest of his drink and bangs the glass on the table and shouts for the waitress. "Gracie! 'Nother!"

A big dude with a tank top and a ZZ Top beard comes strolling over from the back room. He's carrying a tray and wearing an apron around his waist that's barely big enough to reach all the way.

"Gracie? That you?"

She turns and looks at me like she's gonna rip my head off. "Yeah, you got a problem?"

"Shit, no. Just didn't realize you were married."

"Well, I ain't, OK? And right now I got some long haul trucker whose name I don't even remember back at my house lying on the couch doing God knows what to my private things, but I gotta be here, serving you little bitches drinks." She wheels around on Karl and gets right in his face, about six feet, three inches, and easily two hundred and fifty pounds of pissed off waitress turned trucker. "And I better get a damn good tip, too."

Karl leans back and smiles real uncomfortably. "Hey babe, you know it."

"Mmm hmm." Gracie heads back to the bar for his drink.

Danny Boy sets another beer in front of me and takes away the empty. I don't even remember drinking the first one. He says, "Well boys, what's the word?"

Tucker says, "Shit, Danny, we were hoping *you* knew something. TV ain't saying nothin' yet except to tell everybody to stay home."

"That's 'cause they don't know shit neither. Ask me, I say it's their fault. I betchou dollars to doughnuts this is some kinda government thing. Somebody released some kinda gas or somethin' and this is what happened. Or some military bug that was put in our water as an experiment. Just you watch. 'Fore you know it, there'll be roadblocks up and soldiers in hazmat suits runnin' around and martial law and everything."

"Well, I say it's aliens. Billy here thinks I'm fulla shit, but I got proof. Tell 'em what you seen last night, Edgar."

Edgar lifts his dripping muzzle up from his bowl and says, "Last night, I'm heading out to the barn to make sure I latched up the door right…"

Tucker and Danny grin at each other and roll their eyes and Danny Boy mutters, "Typical Browns fan."

"…A-a-a-and there's this flash. The whole sky fills up with this blue light. Then it's gone. Next thing I know, I'm on the floor of the barn wearing this wool coat."

Danny Boy scratches his wife's butt. "Well, that sure does sound like aliens. Shit, Edgar, all these years, I just thought your daddy was a loon, tellin' all them crazy stories about aliens comin' to visit him." Danny Boy thinks on it for a second then says, "But it could just as easily be the government, too. Maybe they're testing some new weapon. One of them non-lethal ones, like the microwave gun. Confuse the enemy and take 'em without firing a shot."

"Maybe it's God." We all look back at Karl. He's drunk already, like normal. He swirls his Cutty and water at us. "Maybe God's punishing y'all. For the way you been to each other."

He's looking at me all weird, like he knows something. All of a sudden, I break out in a sweat. Get real hot and bothered and my face feels like it's on fire. I think about Tina. About the night before. I look at the beer bottle in front of me and I don't much feel like drinking it no more. I imagine her standing there in the kitchen, holding a beer in one hand and the bottle of antifreeze in the other. Measuring it out. Maybe swirling it around a little to mix it up. Gives me the shivers to think about that.

"What about you?" Tucker says. "I suppose God ain't got no beef with you?"

Karl looks down in his glass like there's an answer there. "No, that ain't the case." He points at everybody at the bar, stabs his drink at us accusingly. "But at least you all had somebody nearby when this happened. Least you all weren't alone." He looks down at Edgar and says, "Even you, animal lover."

"Man, if one more person says—"

The door swings open and we all turn and squint against the bright sunlight pouring into our dark little cave. There's a young woman standing there. She doesn't look real sure about coming in and takes a half step back, then thinks better of it and heads on in anyway. She stands near the bar like she's waiting for us to talk.

Danny Boy says, "Can I help you, little miss?"

"Danny? That you? It's me. Kalafat."

"Frank Kalafat? What the hell you doing in *there*, Frank?"

He shuffles his feet and stares at the cruddy floor. "I… made a mistake last night."

"Wait, I recognize you," says Floyd. "Ain't you Don Bunge's daughter, Carrie? Shit, Frank, ain't she your babysitter?"

Frank rubs the back of his neck with his thin, 19-year old hand. "I know," he says. "I couldn't help myself. I didn't mean for it to happen, just did."

I ask him, "Frank, where's your wife at?"

Before he can answer, the door swings open again and the daylight hits him like a police searchlight. "There you are, you two-timing sonuvabitch."

"Missy!" Frank spins on his heels and starts backing up. "Hey, can you believe this stuff? Crazy, huh?"

Missy Kalafat charges in after Frank and they set to running circles through the bar, Missy hollering loud enough to rattle the beer logo pictures in their cheap frames. "You dumb sonuvabitch! Don Bunge's out looking for you right now and he's toting a shotgun and means to shoot you dead! And here I am, only one on our street who's still who I'm supposed to be on account of my two-timing snake of a husband out banging the neighborhood slut instead of being with me! You have no idea how *embarrassing* this is, you slimy bastard!"

"Hey! Take that shit outside, you two!" Danny Boy opens the door for them and Missy Kalafat chases her skinny, teenaged husband outside.

Joe Vickers says, "I think she's liable to kill him 'fore Don Bunge can get around to it."

Tucker shoots a look over at me and my face is burning up again. He looks away real quick.

"Damn, that's fucked up." All I can think to say at the

moment. Everybody just nods their agreement. Not much else you can say. I turn back to Karl and wonder if maybe he's on to something. He looks back at me with watery, drunk eyes.

"This is punishment," he tells me. "God's got Himself a sense of humor."

I wonder who He's punishing, though. And then I get this sneaky suspicion it's me.

"OK, Karl. Time to cut it off." Danny Boy glances up at the neon Miller Lite wall clock. "And it's not even noon yet. That's got to be a record, even for you."

After that, everybody just sits there. All of us staring at our drink of choice like the bottle or glass is gonna pipe up and explain all this to us. That's when the déjà vu hits. That's when I realize that this is what I always do when I ain't got the answer to something. I never talked it out with Tina. I just came down here to drown out the question. I realize that, until this crazy morning, I didn't know shit about what was going on. In my life, in my house. With my wife. What kinda husband don't know his wife's got postpartum depression, or what kinda medicine she's takin'? And then I realize what that burning in my face is. It's shame. Probably with a little guilt mixed in, too. Tina tried to kill me, but as I think about it, I can't hardly blame her at this point. And in the end, she went and accidentally killed herself on account of this crazy switcheroo stuff. Damn right God's got Himself a sense of humor.

The clock hits twelve, and the jukebox back in the corner clicks on. A song starts playing, slow and mournful sounding.

The lyrics hit my brain like a sledgehammer. Something catches in my throat and pricks at the edges of my eyes. I hear Tucker next to me sniffle, and I can see his lips moving. Despite myself, I start mumbling along, too. Didn't even realize I knew this song until the words start falling outta my head.

Tucker looks at me and sings, "Are youuuuu…still miiiiiiiiiiiine?"

Floyd spins on his barstool to face us. "IIIIIIIIIII need your loooooove."

Joe Vickers flips his wife's cheap blond hair back and yells the same up at the ceiling.

Tossing his filthy bar rag over his shoulders, Danny Boy continues the chorus.

All together, we put our arms around each other. We finish the song as one.

And every one of us is crying like a goddamn baby.

* * *

We're driving home in complete silence. No radio, no news. Nothing for almost the whole ride.

Finally, as we're heading up our dirt road, Tucker says, "Dude, what was that all about?"

"I don't know." I snuffle up a gob of snot. "Did we actually sing along to Olivia Newton-John, too?"

"Do me a favor and never mention this to Julia."

"Deal."

Edgar sticks his muzzle through the sliding back window of the cab and starts to sing, "Hopelessly devot—"

"Screw you," Tucker says. "Go hump a sheep."

"You guys are *so* gay."

Great. We're being mocked by livestock.

* * *

Julia's sitting in the middle of a VHS mess in my living room with a pen and legal pad on her lap. Video tapes strewn all over the floor. Little Rico's sitting next to her in his bouncy seat, mesmerized by a row of colorful plastic toys. I feel really envious of the little dude all of a sudden. He don't have no worries at all except for when his next meal's coming and who's gonna take care of the smelly diaper stickin' to his ass.

Julia's mesmerized by the TV. Judge Reinhold and a very young Fred Savage are looking at each other with wide eyes. "These movies are ridiculous," she says.

I look at the cassettes lying around her. "*Vice Versa... 18 Again... Freaky Friday...*"

"None of these movies bother too much to explain what happened. The characters switch bodies, but it's due to the lamest reasons. A magic potion, a magic skull, somebody wishes to be young again. And it's only two characters, not the whole damn town. They spend more screen time on shopping mall montages than on explaining the stupid plot. What a waste of time."

Tucker bends over and snatches up the cover to *Like Father Like Son*. "In a search for answers, you turned to cheesy 80s body switching movies starring Dudley Moore and Kirk Cameron? Did you ask yourself, 'What Would Kirk Cameron Do'?"

Edgar says, "Do you have a wristband with the letters WWKCD?"

"Bite me, lamb chop. I suppose you girls found out all the answers down at McGillicuddy's."

Yeah, you could say I came upon an answer or two.

"Well," Tucker says, "We found out that more folks got hit with the old switcheroo, but not everyone. Karl Klimack and Missy Kalafat were all alone last night and nothin' happened to them."

"So, proximity to another person..." Julia looks sideways at Edgar and keeps going, "or another living thing, definitely has something to do with it."

Tucker says, "Yeah, you had to be close to somebody, I guess."

Little Rico sees me and smiles and starts cooing. Kicking in his seat and pounding his little baby fists against his little baby thighs. He whacks a ring of plastic keys, sends 'em spinning around the bar attached to his seat. His eyes get huge and his mouth hangs open in an amazed Oh My God face.

Julia puts her pad and pen down and looks up at me. It's one of them looks that means what she has to say ain't gonna be something I particularly care to hear. Despite the fact that it's really Tucker's mopey, unshaven mug with those constantly baked-looking, half-closed eyes that are giving me this look, I can still see it in her face.

"Billy..."

"What?" I know what's coming. "Just say it."

"OK. We need to do something about Tina."

"Like what?"

"Well, I think we need to call the police."

Yep, there it is. "Forget it, Julia."

"Billy, you can't leave a dead body in your bedroom. Pretty soon, she's going to start to...you know. Smell."

"What am I going to tell the cops? That my wife killed me? But I *am* my wife now. Her fingerprints are my fingerprints, and whose fingerprints do you think they're gonna find all over that bottle of antifreeze out there?"

"Yeah, but... They'll have to believe you. I mean, look what's going on. They'll have to know."

"But what if they don't, huh? I go to jail. Little Rico will be taken away to some foster home. And the foster mom will probably turn out to be some forty year old guy inside because, oh yeah, God decided it would be funny to play switcheroo with everybody's head. What a gas!"

"What a gas? Are we suddenly in the 1950s now?"

"Fuck you, Tucker! This ain't funny."

"Sorry dude. But no matter how you look at this situation, it really is a little funny. Even in a going-crazy-cartme-off-to-the-nuthouse kinda way."

Julia grabs me by the arm and leads me down the hall toward the bedroom. "Listen. This isn't going to be easy, no matter what you decide to do, but you *have* to do something."

"I know." I'm trying real hard not to cry, but I can feel the tears building up again. My chest gets tight and my nose starts to run. It's something more than just sadness. Feels like five different emotions brimming up and it's weird as hell 'cause there's this distant voice in my brain screaming, 'Be a man and quit your blubbering!' But that voice sounds farther and farther away and the rest of me ain't listening. When I see me lying there and think about Tina, trapped in that worn out, pathetic body, it's too much.

"I can't believe she's gone."

I sit on the bed and cry and Julia rubs my back. She don't say anything, just lets me get it out. And it feels good to do it. Something about being in this body, like I don't have full control over all of the parts, least of all my head. These emotions appear out of nothing, and I can't hold them back. And I was always able to hold them back. Tina even used to bitch that I never cried, not for nothing, even at my dad's funeral. I suppose at one point, I felt like it, but there's no way I woulda done that in front of everyone, in front of the family. In front of the old man. He probably woulda sprung to life outta his casket just to smack me upside the head and yell at me to quit my bellyachin'.

This is so different. So...foreign. But it don't feel wrong, and to be honest, I'm just exhausted. All of a sudden, I just can't fight it no more. It doesn't make any sense to. What's the point of holding it in?

So I cry until I stop. And then I ask Julia, "What if I call the cops and they take me to jail? If that happens, if they come and take Little Rico away, I don't know what

I'll do. It's me in here, but I ain't entirely got a handle on the reins, if you get my meaning."

"Trust me, I get your meaning, and it makes sense. Postpartum depression isn't all up in a woman's head. Her body has gone through lots of changes in the last year, and being a first time mother is very hard. Especially if she feels like she doesn't have much help."

I look at her and she glances kinda sideways when she realizes what she just said. Even she knows what happened here. I feel like a blind fool.

"Look, I know I wasn't the best husband, but I didn't do nothing to her to deserve what I got. Or was going to get. I never beat on her or was mean to her and Rico. I never did anything."

"Maybe that's what the problem was."

Damn, that one hit right between the eyes. Nothing like getting your ass kicked by the truth.

"Billy? Julia?" Tucker calling to us from the living room. "Come out here guys. There's a coupla suits stalking around out in your yard."

Edgar scuttles over to the door and pokes his sheep nose up against the screen. "Oh Jesus, Da-a-a-a-anny Boy was right! The G-Men come to get us!"

PART TWO
Spooks and a Funeral

BLACK SUITS, WHITE shirts, black ties, black shades, standing very official-like out in my front yard. The white dude holds up his credentials and says, "Agent Tim. This here," he points at the black guy, "is Agent Joey."

I try really hard to stifle a laugh, in spite of myself and the situation, but it don't really work. "Agent *Joey*? Are you guys serious? Don't you have official sounding names like Agent Jones and Agent Smith?"

Agent Tim clears his throat and glances around un-comfortably. "The current administration feels our image needs a little softening. We have been directed to give our first names. Simply complying with Bureau regulations, ma'am."

Tucker and Julia are on either side of me, and Edgar's lurking around behind us tugging at some grass. Tucker says, "Are you guys here to tell us what the hell is going on?"

Agent Joey flips through a stack of papers and runs his finger down a list. He says, "We were hoping you might do the same for us. Are you... Julia Denton?"

"Well, yes and no."

"And you," he says turning to Julia. "Are you Tucker Denton?"

"Agent, uh, Joey?" Julia's trying to be polite. "Listen, something strange happened last night. Isn't that the rea-son you guys are out here?"

Agent Tim removes his sunglasses and wipes the lenses. "We are aware of a mysterious...phenomenon which has been widely reported, and we are here to investigate the validity of the claims, Mr. Denton. Perhaps you can start by telling us exactly what happened."

Tucker steps forward and says, "Well, let me put it to you this way. *Mr.* Denton and I, you see, we kinda switched, you know. Mr. Denton there is not really Mr. Denton. He's now Mrs. Denton, and I ain't really Mrs. Denton. I'm now Mr. Denton."

"When we woke up this morning, we realized that we had switched...bodies." Julia pats her Tucker hands on her chest and says, "I'm Julia Denton, on the inside at least."

Agent Joey looks at me and at his list. "Are you Mrs. Tina Gillespie? Is William Gillespie here? Can you verify these claims?"

"Well, I can tell you that I am really Billy, er, William Gillespie. Tina is...she's not feeling well and went to lie down. This has all hit her kinda hard. And our neighbor Edgar is—"

Edgar rams my leg and shakes his sheep head. "Baa!"

"What dude, you have to—"

"BAAA!"

Agent Tim throws out a heavy sigh. "Now folks, please understand that we are not dismissing your claims. There are several leads that we are investigating. It is very hard for us to validate claims such as these. Our ways of identifying citizens include very conventional means like fingerprinting, dental records, photographic ID."

I nudge Edgar and say, "Well, I'm sure our neighbor Edgar could help convince you of this strange occurrence."

Edgar head butts my calf and shakes his stupid sheep head at me again. Looks up at me with pleading sheep eyes.

So I stomp on his sheep foot.

"OW! Dammit, why'd you do that?" He looks up at the Agents and takes a couple steps back. "Oh, shit."

Agents Tim and Joey have clearly just discovered their first piece of concrete evidence, 'cause after a second of shocking realization, they spring into action. Tim pulls out a handheld electronic device and points it at Edgar. Joey yanks a walkie-talkie from his belt and says, "Command, we have a confirmation, repeat verified confirmation at Snow Road, sector four, send containment crew ASAP."

And then they both pull out handguns.

"Whoa," Tucker says backing away. "Hang on there, guys. Ain't no need for all that."

"Remain calm Mrs. Denton. Excuse me, *Mr.* Denton. This is only standard. We have clear regulations for securing a scene and we are simply following those regulations. I assure you that no one will be harmed, as long as you remain compliant."

In the distance, there's a whumping sound. A couple seconds later, a big, black helicopter appears over the treetops and heads straight for us. Dust kicks up into the air from a ways off and a long line of black vehicles comes racing down our lonely dirt road.

I feel a pain in my ankle. "Ow, shit! What the hell Edgar?"

He removes my leg from his mouth and looks up at me with angry sheep eyes. "Now look what you done, dickhead!"

* * *

Demolisher, stuck in the kitty body of Princess Diamond Roses, stands on the top step of the porch and barks at the bewildered agents swarming around the yard. A dozen guys in identical suits and ties and retarded haircuts and black shades scoop soil, take readings on odd-looking devices and shout official sounding commands at each other over their walkie-talkies.

They're over in Edgar's barn, checking out his sheep in an Edgar suit. They're over at Julia and Tucker's, but there ain't much to see over there.

The helicopter has hovered off to some other site. These guys appear to be chasing their tails, what with all the confirmed cases of switcheroo through the town. Can't get 'em to tell us a damn thing about how widespread it is, or how many people have been affected.

Agent Tim stands at the bottom of my front porch stairs watching Demolisher mew-bark and spit at him. "Sir, please control your...animal. I need to gain access to the house to continue my investigation."

Shit. "Why, uh...why do you need to go into the house?"

"Sir, we need to check the entire area to confirm that there are no more victims."

Victims. Nice choice of words. I'm a victim, alright. "Well, there ain't nobody in there but Little Rico, and he's only five months old. But he didn't switch with nobody, least not that I could tell. He's normal as the day he was born."

"Yes, sir, I understand, but I must confirm regardless. Please control your animal, or I will be required to remove it with force."

"Alright dude, chill. No need to go blowing away my cat-dog." I go scoop up Demolisher and tuck his fluffy little body under my arm. "Go ahead, I guess."

And now I'm going to go to jail. I just know it. I look at Tucker and Julia standing out in the yard, but they smile at me. Tucker gives me a quick thumbs up, then goes back to being serious. I mouth at them, *What the fuck?*

"Mr. Gillespie, can you please come in here?"

I clench up and head in. Agent Tim stands in the doorway to my bedroom, but won't go in, just gestures into the room. Sweat breaks out all over Tina's body. I walk over and stick my head in. The bed is made up nice and neat and completely empty. No sign of me anywhere.

"Can you confirm this is your cat?" Agent Tim points to the corner of the room, where Princess Diamond Roses is trying to hover her giant English Mastiff ass over her kitty litter box. She misses and drops a huge turd on the carpet.

"Wh... What?" I'm stunned, and when I'm like that, my brain don't work real well, even if it's Tina's brain I'm currently borrowing.

"Is that your *cat*, sir?"

"Well. It certainly appears to be." I look at Agent Tim and attempt my most innocent-looking smile. "Unless you know of any English Mastiffs that have been trained to crap in a cat box."

"Thank you, sir." He doesn't smile back at me, just lifts his walkie-talkie to his face and says, "Command, Gillespie female-turned-male not on the premises. Considered on the run, locate priority one."

He stomps back outside and Julia and Tucker poke their heads in the front door and both give me the thumbs up again. I feel like I'm gonna faint, but Little Rico starts to cry and I realize it's lunchtime.

I'm sitting at the kitchen table with him when the other two come join me.

"Guys? What the hell did you do?"

"It was my idea," Tucker says. "We hid her. We both agreed with you that it would be best if this just didn't happen right now, not the way we all are. So we moved her."

"Where?"

They just look at each other. Then they stare at the floor.

I'm trying to be calm, but it's not working out too

well. On top of all these weird emotions that I ain't never really bothered dealing with before, now I've got this over-riding sense of fear that, at any moment, a dozen dudes in black suits are gonna bust in and take my newly-female ass to jail for murder. "Tell me. Where…is…she?"

Tucker points past me.

"What, out back?"

He nods his head.

I think my teeth are clenched now 'cause my jaw starts to ache. "You put her outside? Are you fucking nuts?"

He puts a finger to his lips to shush me. "No dude," he whispers. "Not outside. On the back porch. In the… chest freezer."

Now I'm gonna faint. Julia reaches out for Little Rico and I think I hand him to her. I ain't real sure.

'Cause I'm out.

* * *

I'm dreaming, I know it. But it feels so real. More real than real life. Every color jumps out so harsh it hurts to look at stuff. The yellow jumper Little Rico's wearing glows. He's sitting in Tina's lap. They're on the rocking chair. She's got a spit up rag on her shoulder. The blue fabric of the rocker glows in the sunlight through the window. Everything's so sharp and in focus.

Except for Tina. She's gray. She ain't got any color at all. Her eyes are half-closed and she looks like she's about to fall over. I can see individual boogers hanging out of Little Rico's nose, but Tina's face is fuzzy, like I got sleep in my eyes trying to look at her. I rub at 'em and squint, but the harder I look, the more out of focus she is and the more in-focus everything else around her becomes.

I can feel my mouth moving. I'm calling her name, but can't get nothing to come out. Like I'm stuck in a vacuum or something. Like I'm on the other side of thick glass. Like I'm invisible.

She turns her head toward me. I can see the blurry spot where her mouth should be, moving around. Little Rico is cooing and shaking his plastic key ring and I can hear all that, but not her. I'm yelling and straining and nothing comes out, and nothing but silence from her. She's trying to say something to me, I know it, but it ain't getting through. And she just keeps getting more blurred out, like she's disappearing right there.

I rub my eyes again, try to clear away the gunk, but when I open 'em, I'm awake.

* * *

The agents are gone, except for Agent Joey. He's stuck in some black government sedan, sitting out by the road to make sure we don't try to pack up and skip town. Like we're gonna infect somebody or something.

Rico's asleep again, thank God. Poor little dude doesn't deserve this kinda stress. I'm lying on the couch. Tucker and Julia are talking in the kitchen. I hear Edgar's hooves scuffing along the tile floor. I remember when Tina put the tile down, just some cheapo peel-and-stick shit, "Until we can afford the full re-do," she said. For the first time since this happened, I miss her. I feel like she should be just in the other room, but she's not.

She's out in the freezer.

"Tucker?"

"Oh shit, he's awake."

I get up and stumble to the back door. They all come running up behind me. Even Edgar, like he's gonna be of some use in this situation.

I flip open the lid to the chest freezer and stare at my

folded up corpse, resting on top of some deer meat Tina's dad gave us.

"Sonuvabitch. Can't believe I fit in there."

"Yeah, it wasn't easy, especially with them dudes out front. Julia did most of the work, just tossed your body over her shoulder and hauled you right out here."

"Thanks for the play-by-play."

"No problem."

Julia flicks Tucker in the back of the head. "He's being sarcastic, dummy."

"Ow, stop it. I know he's being sarcastic. And I thought you said you'd stop calling me dummy."

"I'll stop calling you dummy when you stop acting like one."

Edgar stomps on the porch and bleats at 'em. "B-A-A-A-A-A! Shut the hell up you two. This ain't the time or place for it."

They look at each other and tell me, "Sorry."

I say, "What am I supposed to do with her now?"

Tucker says, "Yeah, I was thinking about that. Here's what I was thinking... We bury her."

"What?"

"Hear me out, now. We bury her and give her a private little funeral, say what needs to be said and everything, and don't nobody know any different. Just tell them spooks what they already believe, that she run off and you don't know where she went. I mean she did try to murder you, dude. I know it's your wife and you loved her, but given the circumstances..."

"And what happens if everything gets fixed and we all go back to our own bodies? Then it's me down in the ground. Did you think about that?"

Julia, of all people, actually takes Tucker's side here. "Billy, does that really matter? I mean, if we do all switch back, you won't even know it, will you? Technically, you'll be dead."

"Oh man," Edgar says. "This shit makes my head hurt. I'm going to get some grass." He trots down the porch steps and shuffles through the yard with his head down. I kinda feel like doing that too.

"OK, so if we actually did this…if we actually take the now frozen corpse of my former body, which almost certainly contains the mind and soul of my murderous but also apparently postpartumly depressed wife, and we bury it in the ground, where the hell are we going to do that? Out here in my backyard, where there are swarms of government spooks crawling around looking for, um, I don't know, suspicious activity?"

"I got the perfect place," Tucker says. His voice is full of calm, unlike I've heard it yet since he began to inhabit Julia's body. "In my pole barn, back in the corner. We can move the F-150 out of the way and put her there. The whole floor is dirt and when we put the truck back, you'd never know what was there."

"In the ground under your pole barn."

"Yeah."

"Where your broke down, never going to ever run again truck sits."

"Yeah."

"You want my wife's headstone, the marker over her grave, to indicate her final resting place for all of eternity, to be your rusted out, junker Ford pickup truck."

"Well… I wasn't thinking about it in those terms, but…yeah."

What can I do but throw up my hands? "What the hell. Let's do it."

* * *

I stand at the bed looking down at the clothes. My black suit, the only thing I own that didn't come from Steve &

Barry's or Walmart, and a black dress. It's got a white frill along the neckline, which happens to be fairly low. I remember buying it for Tina about a year ago, and how she snorted when she saw it.

She said, "You expect me to *wear* this?"

"No, I expect you to eat it. What's wrong with it?"

"Billy, if I have to *tell* you what's wrong with this dress, then there's no *point* in me telling you because you wouldn't get it anyway."

She always talked like that. It didn't make much sense to me then and it don't make much more sense now. So I put the dress on. Takes me five minutes to realize the stupid thing only has one shoulder strap. The other shoulder is bare. And it's long in the back, but has a really short front that comes up to a slit.

And I can see my underwear.

"Fuck this."

I put the dress on the hanger and stuff it far back into Tina's side of the closet where I found it. The hell with what I'm wearing. I throw on a black Steelers Super Bowl IX shirt. This is a funeral in a pole barn, after all. I put the suit back also. Gonna be kinda hard to pull that thing onto my torso after it's been tucked in the freezer for six hours. Looks like the stuff of my bones will just have to be laid to rest in the stained boxers and torn T-shirt I wore to bed last night.

What does it matter what I wear anyways? Who remembers that shit? There'll be plenty of crazy crap to remember about this particular funeral as it is.

Soon as we agreed on it all, we went to work. I helped dig the hole, though Julia did most of the hard work on account of her Tucker size and strength. That was always the best thing about Tuck. Once he got his mind into something, he could work circles around anybody. Now with Julia's mind in him, they were an unstoppable force.

With only Agent Joey left sittin' in his car at the edge of the yard, at the bottom of the hill where you couldn't see behind the houses too good, it wasn't very hard to sneak around back there. It was still a scary couple minutes, though, carrying my mostly frozen corpse across the yard, but we did it. All them other agents musta found bigger fish to fry 'cause they tore outta there hours ago with the quickness. But to tell the truth, I stopped worrying too much about what else was happening to our little town. Not that I don't care, but the events of the past eighteen hours have all of a sudden caught up to me in a huge rush. I suppose getting ready to shovel dirt on your own body will do that to you.

Tucker, wearing his ratty old moth-eaten Bradshaw jersey that's about three sizes too big on Julia's frame, says, "You think we shoulda left her out for a bit? You know, to thaw?"

"I don't think I could handle watching my body thaw on the floor of your pole barn, Tuck. Bad enough what we're fixing to do right now. I'd just as soon get this over with."

"Yeah, I see what you mean. Sorry, dude."

I look at him and realize, maybe for the first time, that Julia has very large, wide, deeply green eyes. Tucker has her hair pulled back, more for ease than for any sorta style thing. I also realize that, since Tucker took up residence in her, she doesn't seem to have that angry, scrunched up forehead all the time. She doesn't seem pissed every time Tucker comes ambling around in that way that Tucker does. And I remember that she's actually very pretty.

Like Tina back when we first met.

"Tina has blue eyes."

Tucker says, "What?"

I look down at me in the hole. Basically a big square instead of a rectangle, on account of my frozen legs tucked up against my frozen chest like I'm doing a cannonball off a diving board.

"Tina has brown hair and blue eyes. She used to laugh at everything I said. When we first started going out, I swear all we did was laugh."

Julia and Tucker stand alongside me and we all stare down into the hole. We're all sweaty from digging. Edgar moseys up and pokes his head over the edge for a look.

"Tina has blue eyes and brown hair and strong legs. She played volleyball and softball in high school. She could leg press almost a hundred pounds more than me back when we first started going around. She could outrun me, too. It amazed me that we ended up together. I figured if she wanted to, she could take off and I'd never be able to catch up with her.

"I don't remember when we stopped laughing. I think it all just kinda happened at once. One day, we woke up and didn't laugh about nothing. And then we went to the next day and didn't even crack a smile. Is that the way it happens? You just stop laughing one day? A year later, your wife tries to kill you?"

"Yeah," Julia says. "That is how it happens. Except for the whole wife killing you part. I mean the laughing." She looks at Tucker. They stare at each other. "One day we stopped laughing."

"I still laugh," Tucker says.

"I know. It's just not with me anymore."

Tucker puts an arm around Julia and they lean into each other.

I say, "She coulda just left. I don't know why she didn't do that. I'll never know now."

Nobody says a word. I'm not even sure I know what I'm saying. It just pours out.

"I ain't gonna remember her like that. I'm gonna remember when we laughed. I'm gonna write a list of every moment that we spent together laughing. Little stuff, like the time we were out drinking and nowhere near home and it was like midnight and I had to piss like I never had to piss before. Nobody open anywhere in town 'cept the McDonald's drive through. We pull in there and buy the biggest soda they sell and then sit in the parking lot, and I dump all the soda out the window and piss into the cup. That was the greatest piss of my life. Until the cup started to fill up. I was sitting there in the passenger seat of the car, with this really hot and full cup of piss and I couldn't stop going. And Tina was laughing so hard she stopped breathing. One of those laughs where you got your mouth wide open and nothing coming out. Her face was beet red. And that made *me* laugh, and now I got a super-sized cup fulla my own piss, all the way up to the brim and sloshing around, and I can't stop giggling. I put the lid on it and we chucked it out the window as we drove down the road.

"That's the stuff I want to remember."

We're quiet for a long time. After awhile, Edgar says, "A-a-a-a-a-a-men."

"Amen," says Julia.

"Amen," says Tucker.

I say it too. Then I scoop some dirt and toss it in. The dirt hits my left arm and side. I'm burying myself. I toss in another load that jumps off my shoulder and covers part of my face. I toss in another. And another. I bury my head, then my arms. My legs. I cover me up. I work faster. Get into a rhythm. Stop thinking. Just shovel.

In a few minutes, it's done. The hole is gone, just a fresh patch of crumbly earth, and I'm gone, too.

"That's that," I say. I don't know why I say that. We roll the dead F-150 back in place, over the hole.

We stand there for a minute and look at it. In the distance, I hear a low thumping. It's dark outside now, but a sudden flood of light fills the dingy windows of the pole

STEVE LOWE

barn. An amplified voice just outside shouts out, "YOU
IN THERE! WE HAVE THE BARN SURROUND-
ED! COME OUT NOW WITH YOUR HANDS ON
YOUR HEAD."

Sonuvabitch.

* * *

"How did they find out?" Edgar's pacing around on his
stubby little sheep legs, back and forth, going nowhere in
particular. I feel like I'm doing the same thing.

Cornered. Trapped. Busted.

"Oh shit," Tucker says, "we're in so much trouble.
Dude, I can't go to jail like this."

Julia's standing with her arms crossed at her chest. "We
just need to calm down here. We can explain everything
that's happened so far and I don't think any of us are going
to go to jail."

I start to freak out, too. "What are you talking about?
We can't explain shit! Not since the sun came up today.
And now, we're standing here sweaty and dirty with shov-
els in our hands and my body stuffed in a hole underneath
your goddamn truck! What about this scenario does not
scream GOING TO JAIL?"

Edgar stands between the door and us and says, "Hang
on guys. I think I know what this is about. They ain't here
for you."

I say, "Then who the hell are they here for, you?"

"Yeah."

"C'mon Edgar, they wouldn't send a team of federal
agents after you just because you were...you know."

"No, I already told you I wasn't doing that. It's something else."

Tucker steps forward now. "Whatcha mean something
else?"

48

"I've been…experimenting out in the barn."

"Whatcha mean, experimenting out in the barn?"

From outside, the Fed with the bullhorn shouts, "PLACE YOUR WEAPON ON THE GROUND THEN STEP OUTSIDE WITH YOUR FINGERS LACED ON TOP OF YOUR HEAD! YOU HAVE TWO MINUTES TO COMPLY OR WE WILL REMOVE YOU BY FORCE!"

We're all three crowded around our wooly neighbor and waiting for an answer. "I been…trying some stuff out in the barn. With this equipment I found."

Despite her clenched fists and white knuckles, Julia tries the calm, friendly approach. "Edgar, just go ahead and tell us because we need to know what's happening. What experiments, and why do the Feds think you're in here armed to the teeth?"

"U-u-u-u-u-h…" He's wracked by sheep stutters. "Well, my daddy had a buncha stuff up in the attic. Stuff he hid away a long time ago. Y'all remember when he used to say the aliens came here to visit him all them years ago? Well, I guess they left him some stuff to…play with. Or something, I don't know. But I done found it and took it out to the barn. 'Cause I got a two-twenty line out there, you know. I set it up and plugged it in…"

I say, "Edgar, are you telling me alien technology from the 1960s runs on two-twenty electrical current?"

"Uh… I guess so. 'Cause when I plugged her in and turned her on, she came to life."

"Lemme guess, you flipped the switch and the next thing you know, we all done the flip flop."

"No, not quite. Nothing happened. I shut it off and went to bed. Or, at least I thought I shut it off, but then I got to lying there thinking that maybe I forgot. That's when I went out early in the morning, to go unplug it all so's I wouldn't wake up to a burnt down barn. And that's

49

when I saw the big blue flash."

Julia shakes her head, like it's fulla spider webs. "OK, wait. Even if that's what happened, what the hell are the Feds doing here?"

"I don't know! I got scared and buried the machine under a pile of hay when I woke up. I thought they didn't find it when they were in there this afternoon, but they musta figured it out."

"But why do they think you have a *gun*?"

"OK MR. MCGILLICUDDY! YOU'VE BEEN GIVEN YOUR FINAL WARNING. WE ARE NOW AUTHORIZED TO TAKE YOU BY FORCE!"

Tucker looks at me. "McSwillinBuddy? Did they say McSwillinBuddy?"

From the back of the barn there's a harsh, shrill voice, like an air raid siren. "Bring it on you bastards! You ain't takin' me without a fight!"

Danny Boy, in the frumpy 50-year old body of his wife Candace, steps out from the shadows with a Mossberg pump in his swollen, menopausal hands. "This is it, guys! You better find somewheres to hide because this shit is going down!"

Tucker and Edgar and me, we're already runnin' for cover. Julia, she just stands there with this stunned look. "Dan McGillcuddy? Is that you? What the hell is happening?"

"Yeah, it's me, or what's left of me after these government bastards shot me up with their goddamn alien ray! And right now, my wife's swinging from a beam in our basement with a rope around my neck. She couldn't take being trapped in me and seeing my body every time she looked in the mirror! So she killed me! Well, I can't take this shit neither and I mean to get the hell outta here, but they wouldn't let me go! So I shot up Agent Tim's Buick and now they're after me. But they done enough damage.

Now, it's my turn for a little payback."

Outside, there's rustling noises all around the door and the windows. Can't see nothing for the spotlights beaming in, but sure as shit, they're coming. Julia's trying to help, but I see where this is going. I look at Tucker and I can tell he's thinking the same.

Julia says, "Wait, Dan, don't do this! Put the gun down! This is gonna all get figured out, just give it a chance!"

Too late. The rotting front doors of the pole barn smash open and a dozen dudes in black come pouring in. The windows on each side explode and more dudes crash through. All of 'em got rifles and helmets and look like badasses just itching for this sorta deal to go down. Tucker gets to Julia just as Danny Boy raises his shotgun. Tucker, in the skinny frame of his wife's body, flies through the air and levels the solid mass of his own muscle and hair and tattoos.

The last thing I see before the agents slam us to the ground is Danny Boy, bullets riddling him, making his flesh ripple like jello from the impacts, his wife's body convulsing and flying backward through the dusty barn air.

PART THREE
Coming Home

THEY BRING HIM out on a stretcher. Oxygen mask on his face. IV bag hanging next to him. I can't believe it.

"How is he alive? They blasted the hell outta him."

Agent Joey says, "Rubber bullets. Standard procedure in this situation."

Tucker says, "There's a standard procedure for this kinda situation?"

"Well, not with all of these specifics, but yes, when a mentally or emotionally unstable citizen runs the risk of hurting himself or others around him, nonlethal methods are deployed. And his weapon wasn't even loaded anymore. He was pulling a dead trigger before he bolted into the woods and headed this way."

"So, he's not under arrest?"

"No, but he'll be held for observation until more is known about his condition."

Julia says, "And what exactly do you know now about our...condition?"

"I'm sorry ma'am, that's classified at this time." He steps out into the grass before the four of us. "Now folks, we ask that you stay in your homes tonight. Don't go anywhere. There will be agents assigned to every block, so if there's an emergency, we will be here to help. Otherwise, please stay put so we can avoid any more situations. This ended without any major injury to anyone, but the next incident may not. Hopefully, we'll have some answers for you by tomorrow morning."

"And Candace McGillicuddy?" Julia says. "Is she really..."

"Officially, we recovered the body of Daniel McGillicuddy from the basement of the McGillicuddy home this evening. He was unresponsive and was taken to the hospital, where Mrs. Candace McGillicuddy has also been taken for treatment of severe emotional stress and multiple contusions. And that is all the information I have at this time. Now, please, everyone go home. Get some rest. It's been a long day."

* * *

Little Rico's been crying for a while. Poor guy musta heard all the commotion outside. He's wet and hungry and scared. So I clean him up. I feed him. I hold him and rock him and talk to him. I tell him about his mother and about his father.

I don't know which of those I am. I guess I'm both, but I feel like neither. I feel like a husk. This body wrapped around my mind feels loose, like ill-fitting clothes. Like I'm the alien.

I tell Little Rico everything I can remember about his mother. I talk for hours and he snores in the crook of my arm. It's late and I'm nearly passing out with exhaustion. Tucker and Julia went straight home like Agent Joey said. So did Edgar, though he went into the barn instead of his house. For a second, I thought about telling him to switch his machine on again, you know, just in case. Before I could, he turned and looked at me and nodded his sheep head. Like he knew.

I stumble into Little Rico's room and lay him in his crib. I lie down on the floor next to him.

And I sleep.

* * *

I dream.

I'm me again. I got my hands and my arms and everything all back to normal. I take a minute to check and make sure, a quick peek down inside my drawers, a spot check to confirm that my hog and his boys are back where they belong.

I'm in a narrow room. There's a door at one end and a big, wide window in the center. On the other side of the window is another room painted in dark, drabby green. There's a table and two chairs at each end, like the interrogation room in a police station. A cup of coffee steaming on the table, smoky tendrils rising up into the air. Tina's there, sitting in a chair watching the cup steam, but she's not really looking at it. She's staring off into space at something that's not even there.

I bang on the window and shout at her. The glass is thick and doesn't make a sound when I hit it. She can't hear me at all. Just sits there with this worried look on her face. Just sits and waits, fidgets with her hands. Runs her fingers through her hair. Her forehead knitted in a constant frown. Keeps glancing up at a clock on the wall. The hands on the clock don't move, not even the thin second hand. Stuck on 3:24 and 17 seconds.

Must be two-way glass. I get tired of shouting and hitting it and I try the door, but it's locked. The knob won't even jiggle in my hand. I go back to the window and watch her. She crosses and re-crosses her arms and legs. Taps her fingers on the table and bounces her foot on the floor. Waiting, like she knows something's coming, but don't know what or don't know when.

Or maybe that's how *I'm* feeling. Then the door unlocks and swings in.

"Howdy, Billy." A familiar-looking guy enters wearing

a really nice suit, tall with broad shoulders, gleaming white teeth nearly as bright as his shiny, bald head.

"Hi… Terry Bradshaw?"

"Yessiree, atcher service." Terry Bradshaw strides up to me all purposeful and grabs my hand and pumps it hard and fast.

"Terry Bradshaw, why are you here?"

"I was gonna ask you the same, but this here's your dream, ain't it?" Can't argue with that logic.

I say, "OK, just so long as you don't go flashing your ass at me like in that stupid Matthew McConaughey movie you were in."

He laughs real quick, then his face goes dead serious. "That's funny. You're a real comedian. What the hell were you doing watching that anyway? You a queer or something?"

"Well…no, I…my wife wanted to see it, so, you know…"

"Ah, uh huh. Sure." He points at the window. "That there your wife?"

"Yeah, that's Tina. I need to talk to her. Can you let me in with her?"

"Oh, no. You're not allowed to go in there. Got to have the proper clearance."

"Then can you at least tell me what's she doing in there?"

He gives me this sorta shocked look. "Whaddaya mean, what's she doing in there? They've got questions that need answers, that's what. She's in some trouble."

"What trouble? What's going on here?"

He turns to face me and puts a huge, battered, arthritic quarterback hand on my shoulder. His suit is gone and he's dressed in a big yellow nightshirt that comes down to his knees and he's got a bright yellow sleeping cap on his head. "Don't tell me you done forgot everything that's goin' on. What she done to you?"

I watch her again through the window. She looks around, more worried than before. Seems like she's about to cry. I see guilt and sadness in her sparkling eyes. "No, I ain't forgot."

I turn back to him and Terry Bradshaw has his shirt off and he's breastfeeding Little Rico. I say, "Listen, I know something bad happened, but I don't care. It ain't all her fault. In fact, I feel like it's more mine than hers anyways. I ain't mad at her."

Terry shifts Little Rico around to the other side and says, "Well, that really ain't up to you to decide, is it?"

"I don't know. I don't know nothing no more. I don't even understand what happened last night."

"Well, that part's easy."

"Wait, you know how we got switched?"

Little Rico's gone now and Terry Bradshaw is wearing a red velvet smoking jacket and has a giant, green parrot sitting on his shoulder. "Yes I do. It was the government. And they mean to switch y'all back tonight, 'round about the same time. Least that's the plan. But you know the government. Don't nothing go according to plan!" He smacks his meaty paw up against my arm and laughs.

"Damn, Danny Boy was right. Edgar thought it was aliens, but it *was* the government."

"Oh, they're both right."

"What? How?"

"Edgar turned on his machine, but the Feds already had theirs running, for something like thirty years. It was just waiting for the right signal from the other. Suppose now they'll just throw the switch in the other direction."

"So it was the Feds AND aliens that turned us?"

"Well, yes and no. Don't forget about God."

Even for a dream, this is making my head swim. "What

about God? I don't understand."

"Where do you think the big blue light in the sky come from?"

I shake my head like I don't know, 'cause I don't. Now Terry Bradshaw's wearing a rusty suit of armor and nods his head back at me. The creaky metal helmet squeaks.

I say, "That don't fit."

"It's not too bad, just a little tight around the crotch, if you catch my drift." He slides a metal hand between his thighs and shoots me a wink.

"No, I mean about what you said."

"Oh, yeah, that. You're right. None of it fits. And it all fits. Just like it should."

I watch Tina again. She's up and pacing. She walks by the window and stares through the glass at me, brushes a strand of hair off her forehead. Feels like she's looking right in my eyes. I know she can't see me through the two-way glass because she doesn't ever look at me like that anymore. She won't let me see in her eyes, like I'm gonna notice something there that she don't want me to see. Or maybe it's me who doesn't want to see it there.

"Look, I got to head off." Terry Bradshaw is dressed in his suit again. The yellow sleeping cap is back on his head. "I need to get to the studio. It's Sunday and we got football to talk about, and if I show up late, Howie sits on my head and farts during the breaks."

Terry Bradshaw turns and heads for the door. He says over his shoulder as he walks out, "Take it easy, dude. Catch ya on the flip side."

"Bye, Terry Bradshaw."

Tina turns away from the window and sits back down in her chair. I gotta go, too. I lean up against the window. My breath makes a cloud on the glass. I say, "Bye, Tina."

That's when I wake up.

* * *

Where am I?

On the floor in Rico's room. I can hear him breathing. His tiny little snore. Silver moonlight through the window makes a rectangle on the carpet. I see stuffed animals in the corner. The rocking chair. One of Tina's nursing bras slung over the back of it.

It's early, maybe two or three in the morning. The moon's getting low in the sky, will be setting soon, as it does this time of year.

I stumble into the bathroom and fish through my drawers for my plumbing. I have the strongest sense of déjà vu. I've been here before and done this already. I say the hell with it and pop a squat and do my thing, and while I sit there it all hits me again in a rush.

I ain't in the dream no more. I'm back. I'm in that other dream again, the one where I'm Tina and Tina's me. And I'm dead and buried and covered by a rusting hunk of junk in my neighbor's barn and I'm a depressed mother who's now a widow and a widower at the same time. I feel like I've lost a wife and a husband, 'cause when you get right down to it, that's what happened. I ain't Tina, but I ain't me either. Not anymore. Not never again.

I'm no one.

I'm the only person Little Rico's got left in this whole world.

I check on him again but my brain's on cruise control. I ain't driving, just along for the ride. This body takes me through the house, down the hall, past my bedroom. Take a quick peek in at the empty bed where everything changed just about 24 hours ago.

Glide on down the hall, out the front door, down the porch steps. The air is cool and my breath plumes out

61

ahead of me. The grass is wet and icy under my feet. It ain't nearly as long as it was, thanks to Edgar. I stand out in the middle of the lawn and turn my face up to the semicircle of moon. And right at that moment, I know. It all adds up, makes sense to me. Under the muted glow of the metallic moon, I understand.

I close my eyes and imagine I see her, walking across the yard toward me. She's her and I'm me again. I know it's just a mirage, that she ain't really there, but I smile at her all the same. And she smiles back at me, just like she used to. Like I remember. I spread my arms open wide for her. She don't turn away. She opens up her arms too, and folds me into her.

I say, "Hey baby. I missed you. Welcome home."

I look up in the sky and the shining moon disappears in a flash of the deepest blue light.

ABOUT THE AUTHOR

Steve Lowe has never been mistaken for a woman, or at least, not to his face. When he's not ruining his kids' lives or avoiding his wife's plans to completely rebuild their home, he's probably covering a sporting event somewhere. And if he's not doing any of those things, he's off hiding with his laptop, causing trouble on the Internet. You can find him there at http://steve-lowe.com

Bizarro books

CATALOG   SPRING 2010

Bizarro Books publishes under the following imprints:

www.rawdogscreamingpress.com

www.eraserheadpress.com

www.afterbirthbooks.com

www.swallowdownpress.com

For all your Bizarro needs visit:

WWW.BIZARROCENTRAL.COM

Introduce yourselves to the bizarro genre and all of its authors with the Bizarro Starter Kit series. Each volume features short novels and short stories by ten of the leading bizarro authors, designed to give you a perfect sampling of the genre for only $5 plus shipping.

BB-0X1
"The Bizarro Starter Kit"
(Orange)

Featuring D. Harlan Wilson, Carlton Mellick III, Jeremy Robert Johnson, Kevin L Donihe, Gina Ranalli, Andre Duza, Vincent W. Sakowski, Steve Beard, John Edward Lawson, and Bruce Taylor.

236 pages $5

BB-0X2
"The Bizarro Starter Kit"
(Blue)

Featuring Ray Fracalossy, Jeremy C. Shipp, Jordan Krall, Mykle Hansen, Andersen Prunty, Eckhard Gerdes, Bradley Sands, Steve Aylett, Christian TeBordo, and Tony Rauch.

244 pages $5

BB-001 "The Kafka Effekt" D. Harlan Wilson - A collection of forty-four irreal short stories loosely written in the vein of Franz Kafka, with more than a pinch of William S. Burroughs sprinkled on top. **211 pages $14**

BB-002 "Satan Burger" Carlton Mellick III - The cult novel that put Carlton Mellick III on the map ... Six punks get jobs at a fast food restaurant owned by the devil in a city violently overpopulated by surreal alien cultures. **236 pages $14**

BB-003 "Some Things Are Better Left Unplugged" Vincent Sakwoski - Join The Man and his Nemesis, the obese tabby, for a nightmare roller coaster ride into this postmodern fantasy. **152 pages $10**

BB-004 "Shall We Gather At the Garden?" Kevin L Donihe - Donihe's Debut novel. Midgets take over the world, The Church of Lionel Richie vs. The Church of the Byrds, plant porn and more! **244 pages $14**

BB-005 "Razor Wire Pubic Hair" Carlton Mellick III - A genderless humandildo is purchased by a razor dominatrix and brought into her nightmarish world of bizarre sex and mutilation. **176 pages $11**

BB-006 "Stranger on the Loose" D. Harlan Wilson - The fiction of Wilson's 2nd collection is planted in the soil of normalcy, but what grows out of that soil is a dark, witty, otherworldly jungle... **228 pages $14**

BB-007 "The Baby Jesus Butt Plug" Carlton Mellick III - Using clones of the Baby Jesus for anal sex will be the hip sex fetish of the future. **92 pages $10**

BB-008 "Fishyfleshed" Carlton Mellick III - The world of the past is an illogical flatland lacking in dimension and color, a sick-scape of crispy squid people wandering the desert for no apparent reason. **260 pages $14**

BB-009 "Dead Bitch Army" Andre Duza - Step into a world filled with racist teenagers, cannibals, 100 warped Uncle Sams, automobiles with razor-sharp teeth, living graffiti, and a pissed-off zombie bitch out for revenge. 344 pages $16

BB-010 "The Menstruating Mall" Carlton Mellick III - "The Breakfast Club meets Chopping Mall as directed by David Lynch." - Brian Keene 212 pages $12

BB-011 "Angel Dust Apocalypse" Jeremy Robert Johnson - Meth-heads, man-made monsters, and murderous Neo-Nazis. "Seriously amazing short stories..." - Chuck Palahniuk, author of Fight Club 184 pages $11

BB-012 "Ocean of Lard" Kevin L Donihe / Carlton Mellick III - A parody of those old Choose Your Own Adventure kid's books about some very odd pirates sailing on a sea made of animal fat. 176 pages $12

BB-013 "Last Burn in Hell" John Edward Lawson - From his lurid angst-affair with a lesbian music diva to his ascendance as unlikely pop icon the one constant for Kenrick Brimley, official state prison gigolo, is he's got no clue what he's doing. 172 pages $14

BB-014 "Tangerinephant" Kevin Dole 2 - TV-obsessed aliens have abducted Michael Tangerinephant in this bizarro combination of science fiction, satire, and surrealism. 164 pages $11

BB-015 "Foop!" Chris Genoa - Strange happenings are going on at Dactyl, Inc, the world's first and only time travel tourism company.
"A surreal pie in the face!" - Christopher Moore 300 pages $14

BB-016 "Spider Pie" Alyssa Sturgill - A one-way trip down a rabbit hole inhabited by sexual deviants and friendly monsters, fairytale beginnings and hideous endings. 104 pages $11

BB-017 "The Unauthorized Woman" Efrem Emerson - Enter the world of the inner freak, a landscape populated by the pre-dead and morticioners, by cockroaches and 300-lb robots. **104 pages $11**

BB-018 "Fugue XXIX" Forrest Aguirre - Tales from the fringe of speculative literary fiction where innovative minds dream up the future's uncharted territories while mining forgotten treasures of the past. **220 pages $16**

BB-019 "Pocket Full of Loose Razorblades" John Edward Lawson - A collection of dark bizarro stories. From a giant rectum to a foot-fungus factory to a girl with a biforked tongue. **190 pages $13**

BB-020 "Punk Land" Carlton Mellick III - In the punk version of Heaven, the anarchist utopia is threatened by corporate fascism and only Goblin, Mortician's sperm, and a blue-mohawked female assassin named Shark Girl can stop them. **284 pages $15**

BB-021 "Pseudo-City" D. Harlan Wilson - Pseudo-City exposes what waits in the bathroom stall, under the manhole cover and in the corporate boardroom, all in a way that can only be described as mind-bogglingly irreal. **220 pages $16**

BB-022 "Kafka's Uncle and Other Strange Tales" Bruce Taylor - Anslenot and his giant tarantula (tormentor? fri-end?) wander a desecrated world in this novel and collection of stories from Mr. Magic Realism Himself. **348 pages $17**

BB-023 "Sex and Death In Television Town" Carlton Mellick III - In the old west, a gang of hermaphrodite gunslingers take refuge from a demon plague in Telos: a town where its citizens have televisions instead of heads. **184 pages $12**

BB-024 "It Came From Below The Belt" Bradley Sands - What can Grover Goldstein do when his severed, sentient penis forces him to return to high school and help it win the presidential election? **204 pages $13**

BB-025 "Sick: An Anthology of Illness" John Lawson, editor - These Sick stories are horrendous and hilarious dissections of creative minds on the scalpel's edge. **296 pages $16**

BB-026 "Tempting Disaster" John Lawson, editor - A shocking and alluring anthology from the fringe that examines our culture's obsession with taboos. **260 pages $16**

BB-027 "Siren Promised" Jeremy Robert Johnson & Alan M Clark - Nominated for the Bram Stoker Award. A potent mix of bad drugs, bad dreams, brutal bad guys, and surreal/incredible art by Alan M. Clark. **190 pages $13**

BB-028 "Chemical Gardens" Gina Ranalli - Ro and punk band Green is the Enemy find Kreepkins, a surfer-dude warlock, a vengeful demon, and a Metal Priestess in their way as they try to escape an underground nightmare. **188 pages $13**

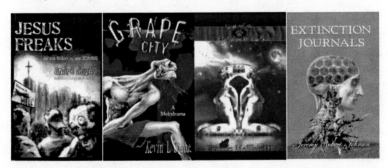

BB-029 "Jesus Freaks" Andre Duza - For God so loved the world that he gave his only two begotten sons… and a few million zombies. **400 pages $16**

BB-030 "Grape City" Kevin L. Donihe - More Donihe-style comedic bizarro about a demon named Charles who is forced to work a minimum wage job on Earth after Hell goes out of business. **108 pages $10**

BB-031"Sea of the Patchwork Cats" Carlton Mellick III - A quiet dreamlike tale set in the ashes of the human race. For Mellick enthusiasts who also adore The Twilight Zone. **112 pages $10**

BB-032 "Extinction Journals" Jeremy Robert Johnson - An uncanny voyage across a newly nuclear America where one man must confront the problems associated with loneliness, insane dieties, radiation, love, and an ever-evolving cockroach suit with a mind of its own. **104 pages $10**

  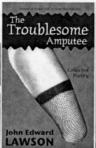 

BB-033 "Meat Puppet Cabaret" Steve Beard - At last! The secret connection between Jack the Ripper and Princess Diana's death revealed! **240 pages $16 / $30**

BB-034 "The Greatest Fucking Moment in Sports" Kevin L. Donihe - In the tradition of the surreal anti-sitcom Get A Life comes a tale of triumph and agape love from the master of comedic bizarro. **108 pages $10**

BB-035 "The Troublesome Amputee" John Edward Lawson - Disturbing verse from a man who truly believes nothing is sacred and intends to prove it. **104 pages $9**

BB-036 "Deity" Vic Mudd - God (who doesn't like to be called "God") comes down to a typical, suburban, Ohio family for a little vacation—but it doesn't turn out to be as relaxing as He had hoped it would be... **168 pages $12**

BB-037 "The Haunted Vagina" Carlton Mellick III - It's difficult to love a woman whose vagina is a gateway to the world of the dead. **132 pages $10**

BB-038 "Tales from the Vinegar Wasteland" Ray Fracalossy - Witness: a man is slowly losing his face, a neighbor who periodically screams out for no apparent reason, and a house with a room that doesn't actually exist. **240 pages $14**

BB-039 "Suicide Girls in the Afterlife" Gina Ranalli - After Pogue commits suicide, she unexpectedly finds herself an unwilling "guest" at a hotel in the Afterlife, where she meets a group of bizarre characters, including a goth Satan, a hippie Jesus, and an alien-human hybrid. **100 pages $9**

BB-040 "And Your Point Is?" Steve Aylett - In this follow-up to LINT multiple authors provide critical commentary and essays about Jeff Lint's mind-bending literature. **104 pages $11**

BB-041 "Not Quite One of the Boys" Vincent Sakowski - While drug-dealer Maxi drinks with Dante in purgatory, God and Satan play a little tri-level chess and do a little bargaining over his business partner, Vinnie, who is still left on earth. **220 pages $14**

BB-042 "Teeth and Tongue Landscape" Carlton Mellick III - On a planet made out of meat, a socially-obsessive monophobic man tries to find his place amongst the strange creatures and communities that he comes across. **110 pages $10**

BB-043 "War Slut" Carlton Mellick III - Part "1984," part "Waiting for Godot," and part action horror video game adaptation of John Carpenter's "The Thing." **116 pages $10**

BB-044 "All Encompassing Trip" Nicole Del Sesto - In a world where coffee is no longer available, the only television shows are reality TV re-runs, and the animals are talking back, Nikki, Amber and a singing Coyote in a do-rag are out to restore the light **308 pages $15**

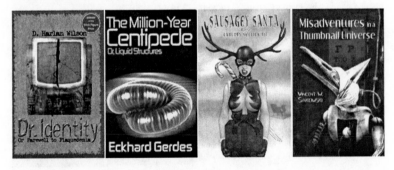

BB-045 "Dr. Identity" D. Harlan Wilson - Follow the Dystopian Duo on a killing spree of epic proportions through the irreal postcapitalist city of Bliptown where time ticks sideways, artificial Bug-Eyed Monsters punish citizens for consumer-capitalist lethargy, and ultraviolence is as essential as a daily multivitamin. **208 pages $15**

BB-046 "The Million-Year Centipede" Eckhard Gerdes - Wakelin, frontman for 'The Hinge,' wrote a poem so prophetic that to ignore it dooms a person to drown in blood. **130 pages $12**

BB-047 "Sausagey Santa" Carlton Mellick III - A bizarro Christmas tale featuring Santa as a piratey mutant with a body made of sausages. 124 pages $10

BB-048 "Misadventures in a Thumbnail Universe" Vincent Sakowski - Dive deep into the surreal and satirical realms of neo-classical Blender Fiction, filled with television shoes and flesh-filled skies. **120 pages $10**

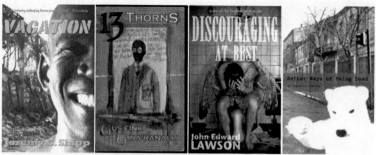

BB-049 **"Vacation" Jeremy C. Shipp** - Blueblood Bernard Johnson leaved his boring life behind to go on The Vacation, a year-long corporate sponsored odyssey. But instead of seeing the world, Bernard is captured by terrorists, becomes a key figure in secret drug wars, and, worse, doesn't once miss his secure American Dream. **160 pages $14**

BB-051 **"13 Thorns" Gina Ranalli** - Thirteen tales of twisted, bizarro horror. **240 pages $13**

BB-050 **"Discouraging at Best" John Edward Lawson** - A collection where the absurdity of the mundane expands exponentially creating a tidal wave that sweeps reason away. For those who enjoy satire, bizarro, or a good old-fashioned slap to the senses. **208 pages $15**

BB-052 **"Better Ways of Being Dead" Christian TeBordo** - In this class, the students have to keep one palm down on the table at all times, and listen to lectures about a panda who speaks Chinese. **216 pages $14**

BB-053 **"Ballad of a Slow Poisoner" Andrew Goldfarb** Millford Mutterwurst sat down on a Tuesday to take his afternoon tea, and made the unpleasant discovery that his elbows were becoming flatter. **128 pages $10**

BB-054 **"Wall of Kiss" Gina Ranalli** - A woman... A wall... Sometimes love blooms in the strangest of places. **108 pages $9**

BB-055 **"HELP! A Bear is Eating Me" Mykle Hansen** - The bizarro, heartwarming, magical tale of poor planning, hubris and severe blood loss... **150 pages $11**

BB-056 **"Piecemeal June" Jordan Krall** - A man falls in love with a living sex doll, but with love comes danger when her creator comes after her with crab-squid assassins. **90 pages $9**

BB-057 **"Laredo" Tony Rauch** - Dreamlike, surreal stories by Tony Rauch. **180 pages $12**

BB-058 **"The Overwhelming Urge" Andersen Prunty** - A collection of bizarro tales by Andersen Prunty. **150 pages $11**

BB-059 **"Adolf in Wonderland" Carlton Mellick III** - A dreamlike adventure that takes a young descendant of Adolf Hitler's design and sends him down the rabbit hole into a world of imperfection and disorder. **180 pages $11**

BB-060 **"Super Cell Anemia" Duncan B. Barlow** - "Unrelentingly bizarre and mysterious, unsettling in all the right ways..." - Brian Evenson. **180 pages $12**

BB-061 **"Ultra Fuckers" Carlton Mellick III** - Absurdist suburban horror about a couple who enter an upper middle class gated community but can't find their way out. **108 pages $9**

BB-062 **"House of Houses" Kevin L. Donihe** - An odd man wants to marry his house. Unfortunately, all of the houses in the world collapse at the same time in the Great House Holocaust. Now he must travel to House Heaven to find his departed fiancee. **172 pages $11**

BB-063 **"Necro Sex Machine" Andre Duza** - The Dead Bitch returns in this follow-up to the bizarro zombie epic Dead Bitch Army. **400 pages $16**

BB-064 **"Squid Pulp Blues" Jordan Krall** - In these three bizarro-noir novellas, the reader is thrown into a world of murderers, drugs made from squid parts, deformed gun-toting veterans, and a mischievous apocalyptic donkey. **204 pages $12**

BB-065 **"Jack and Mr. Grin" Andersen Prunty** - "When Mr. Grin calls you can hear a smile in his voice. Not a warm and friendly smile, but the kind that seizes your spine in fear. You don't need to pay your phone bill to hear it. That smile is in every line of Prunty's prose." - Tom Bradley. **208 pages $12**

BB-066 **"Cybernetrix" Carlton Mellick III** - What would you do if your normal everyday world was slowly mutating into the video game world from Tron? **212 pages $12**

BB-067 **"Lemur" Tom Bradley** - Spencer Sproul is a would-be serial-killing bus boy who can't manage to murder, injure, or even scare anybody. However, there are other ways to do damage to far more people and do it legally... **120 pages $12**

BB-068 **"Cocoon of Terror" Jason Earls** - Decapitated corpses...a sculpture of terror...Zelian's masterpiece, his Cocoon of Terror, will trigger a supernatural disaster for everyone on Earth. **196 pages $14**

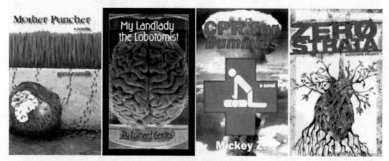

BB-069 **"Mother Puncher" Gina Ranalli** - The world has become tragically over-populated and now the government strongly opposes procreation. Ed is employed by the government as a mother-puncher. He doesn't relish his job, but he knows it has to be done and he knows he's the best one to do it. **120 pages $9**

BB-070 **"My Landlady the Lobotomist" Eckhard Gerdes** - The brains of past tenants line the shelves of my boarding house, soaking in a mysterious elixir. One more slip-up and the landlady might just add my frontal lobe to her collection. **116 pages $12**

BB-071 **"CPR for Dummies" Mickey Z.** - This hilarious freakshow at the world's end is the fragmented, sobering debut novel by acclaimed nonfiction author Mickey Z. **216 pages $14**

BB-072 **"Zerostrata" Andersen Prunty** - Hansel Nothing lives in a tree house, suffers from memory loss, has a very eccentric family, and falls in love with a woman who runs naked through the woods every night. **144 pages $11**

BB-073 "The Egg Man" Carlton Mellick III - It is a world where humans reproduce like insects. Children are the property of corporations, and having an enormous ten-foot brain implanted into your skull is a grotesque sexual fetish. Mellick's industrial urban dystopia is one of his darkest and grittiest to date. **184 pages $11**

BB-074 "Shark Hunting in Paradise Garden" Cameron Pierce - A group of strange humanoid religious fanatics travel back in time to the Garden of Eden to discover it is invested with hundreds of giant flying maneating sharks. **150 pages $10**

BB-075 "Apeshit" Carlton Mellick III - Friday the 13th meets Visitor Q. Six hipster teens go to a cabin in the woods inhabited by a deformed killer. An incredibly fucked-up parody of B-horror movies with a bizarro slant. **192 pages $12**

BB-076 "Rampaging Fuckers of Everything on the Crazy Shitting Planet of the Vomit At smosphere" Mykle Hansen - 3 bizarro satires. Monster Cocks, Journey to the Center of Agnes Cuddlebottom, and Crazy Shitting Planet. **228 pages $12**

BB-077 "The Kissing Bug" Daniel Scott Buck - In the tradition of Roald Dahl, Tim Burton, and Edward Gorey, comes this bizarro anti-war children's story about a bohemian conenose kissing bug who falls in love with a human woman. **116 pages $10**

BB-078 "MachoPoni" Lotus Rose - It's My Little Pony... *Bizarro* style! A long time ago Poniworld was split in two. On one side of the Jagged Line is the Pastel Kingdom, a magical land of music, parties, and positivity. On the other side of the Jagged Line is Dark Kingdom inhabited by an army of undead ponies. **148 pages $11**

BB-079 "The Faggiest Vampire" Carlton Mellick III - A Roald Dahl-esque children's story about two faggy vampires who partake in a mustache competition to find out which one is truly the faggiest. **104 pages $10**

BB-080 "Sky Tongues" Gina Ranalli - The autobiography of Sky Tongues, the biracial hermaphrodite actress with tongues for fingers. Follow her strange life story as she rises from freak to fame. **204 pages $12**

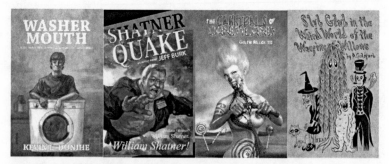

BB-081 **"Washer Mouth" Kevin L. Donihe** - A washing machine becomes human and pursues his dream of meeting his favorite soap opera star. **244 pages $11**

BB-082 **"Shatnerquake" Jeff Burk** - All of the characters ever played by William Shatner are suddenly sucked into our world. Their mission: hunt down and destroy the real William Shatner. **100 pages $10**

BB-083 **"The Cannibals of Candyland" Carlton Mellick III** - There exists a race of cannibals that are made of candy. They live in an underground world made out of candy. One man has dedicated his life to killing them all. **170 pages $11**

BB-084 **"Slub Glub in the Weird World of the Weeping Willows" Andrew Goldfarb** - The charming tale of a blue glob named Slub Glub who helps the weeping willows whose tears are flooding the earth. There are also hyenas, ghosts, and a voodoo priest **100 pages $10**

BB-085 **"Super Fetus" Adam Pepper** - Try to abort this fetus and he'll kick your ass! **104 pages $10**

BB-086 **"Fistful of Feet" Jordan Krall** - A bizarro tribute to spaghetti westerns, featuring Cthulhu-worshipping Indians, a woman with four feet, a crazed gunman who is obsessed with sucking on candy, Syphilis-ridden mutants, sexually transmitted tattoos, and a house devoted to the freakiest fetishes. **228 pages $12**

BB-087 **"Ass Goblins of Auschwitz" Cameron Pierce** - It's Monty Python meets Nazi exploitation in a surreal nightmare as can only be imagined by Bizarro author Cameron Pierce. **104 pages $10**

BB-088 **"Silent Weapons for Quiet Wars" Cody Goodfellow** - "This is high-end psychological surrealist horror meets bottom-feeding low-life crime in a techno-thrilling science fiction world full of Lovecraft and magic..." -John Skipp **212 pages $12**

BB-089 "Warrior Wolf Women of the Wasteland" Carlton Mellick III
Road Warrior Werewolves versus McDonaldland Mutants...post-apocalyptic fiction has never been quite like this. **316 pages $13**

BB-090 "Cursed" Jeremy C Shipp - The story of a group of characters who believe they are cursed and attempt to figure out who cursed them and why. A tale of stylish absurdism and suspenseful horror. **218 pages $15**

BB-091 "Super Giant Monster Time" Jeff Burk - A tribute to choose your own adventures and Godzilla movies. Will you escape the giant monsters that are rampaging the fuck out of your city and shit? Or will you join the mob of alien-controlled punk rockers causing chaos in the streets? What happens next depends on you. **188 pages $12**

BB-092 "Perfect Union" Cody Goodfellow - "Cronenberg's THE FLY on a grand scale: human/insect gene-spliced body horror, where the human hive politics are as shocking as the gore." -John Skipp. **272 pages $13**

BB-093 "Sunset with a Beard" Carlton Mellick III - 14 stories of surreal science fiction. **200 pages $12**

BB-094 "My Fake War" Andersen Prunty - The absurd tale of an unlikely soldier forced to fight a war that, quite possibly, does not exist. It's Rambo meets Waiting for Godot in this subversive satire of American values and the scope of the human imagination. **128 pages $11**

BB-095"Lost in Cat Brain Land" Cameron Pierce - Sad stories from a surreal world. A fascist mustache, the ghost of Franz Kafka, a desert inside a dead cat. Primordial entities mourn the death of their child. The desperate serve tea to mysterious creatures. A hopeless romantic falls in love with a pterodactyl. And much more. **152 pages $11**

BB-096 "The Kobold Wizard's Dildo of Enlightenment +2" Carlton Mellick III - A Dungeons and Dragons parody about a group of people who learn they are only made up characters in an AD&D campaign and must find a way to resist their nerdy teenaged players and retarded dungeon master in order to survive. **232 pages $12**

BB-097 **"My Heart Said No, but the Camera Crew Said Yes!"** Bradley
Sands - A collection of short stories that are crammed with the delightfully odd and the
scurrilously silly. **140 pages $13**

BB-098 **"A Hundred Horrible Sorrows of Ogner Stump"** Andrew
Goldfarb - Goldfarb's acclaimed comic series. A magical and weird journey into
the horrors of everyday life. **164 pages $11**

BB-099 **"Pickled Apocalypse of Pancake Island"** Cameron Pierce
A demented fairy tale about a pickle, a pancake, and the apocalypse. **102 pages $8**

BB-100 **"Slag Attack"** Andersen Prunty - Slag Attack features four visceral,
noir stories about the living, crawling apocalypse. A slag is what survivors are calling the
slug-like maggots raining from the sky, burrowing inside people, and hollowing out their
flesh and their sanity. **148 pages $11**

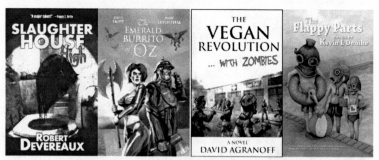

BB-101 **"Slaughterhouse High"** Robert Devereaux - A place where
schools are built with secret passageways, rebellious teens get zippers installed in their
mouths and genitals, and once a year, on that special night, one couple is slaughtered and
the bits of their bodies are kept as souvenirs. **304 pages $13**

BB-102 **"The Emerald Burrito of Oz"** John Skipp & Marc Levinthal
OZ IS REAL! Magic is real! The gate is really in Kansas! And America is finally allowing
Earth tourists to visit this weird-ass, mysterious land. But when Gene of Los Angeles heads off
for summer vacation in the Emerald City, little does he know that a war is brewing...a war that
could destroy both worlds. **280 pages $13**

BB-103 **"The Vegan Revolution... with Zombies"** David Agranoff
When there's no more meat in hell, the vegans will walk the earth. **160 pages $11**

BB-104 **"The Flappy Parts"** Kevin L Donihe - Poems about bunnies, LSD,
and police abuse. You know, things that matter. **132 pages $11**